"Come back soon!" called Possum when the rain

was over. "My home is your home!"

"Come in!" cried Possum. The wind blew, the rain poured, and the animals watched, snug and dry, from Possum's new home.

They all stood back.

"Oh, Papa, it's the most beautiful home in the world!" exclaimed the little possums.

"How can we ever thank you?" Possum asked the animals. "We could never have done it without you."

Thunder rumbled.

The oriole wove hammock-like nests of grasses and vines in the tree above the house.

As they stood admiring the wasp's delicate handiwork, an oriole flew in. "I heard there was some building going on and thought you might need my help," he sang. "Everyone knows a nest is best! Why sleep on the damp ground when you could swing in a nest! Let me show you!"

A wasp flew by. "What's happening here?" she buzzed.

"Possum's brush pile washed away," answered the muskrat. "He needs help building a new home."

"I can make a comb of chewed wood and saliva. It might make nice windows," said the wasp, and she set to work.

Muskrat followed them up the rise
and showed the possums how to build a
dome of reeds and mud over the burrow
that the chipmunk had helped them dig.

"Hello, Muskrat," he called. "How did you come by such a nice house?"

"It's a lodge!" called the muskrat. "And I built it myself. Cattails and mud! Want me to show you?"

Possum and his children walked down to the marsh
in search of a home. They found a nice one—
occupied, unfortunately.

"Look at our new home, Papa!" cried the little possums when Possum returned.

Possum looked at the door hole in dismay. "I'm sure its lovely in there," he said sadly, "but I will never fit, I'm afraid."

"Oh dear," said the chipmunk. "I can see that now. Well, perhaps you could use it as a basement."

The possums followed the chipmunk
up to higher ground. She sent Possum to
gather dry leaves for bedding while she
and the little possums set to digging.

Possum climbed down. A chipmunk hopped by. "Where's your brush pile?" she squeaked.

"Gone," sighed Possum, "washed away."

"Oh! Bad luck," the chipmunk sympathized. "I could help you dig a new home," she offered.

"Dig?" he asked.

"Yes, you know," she said. "We'll dig a bedroom, bathroom, larder . . ."

Possum's eyes widened. "Yes," said Possum. "That sounds very nice."

There was not a brush pile in sight. He was good at gathering
leaves . . . but a leaf pile was not enough.

"Don't worry, children," he said. "We'll find a new home."

"Oh, Papa, our home is gone!" cried the young possums.

"Where will we live? Where will we sleep?"

Possum surveyed the soggy land below.

"Hang on tight, children!" Possum yelled as their brush pile home was swept downstream.

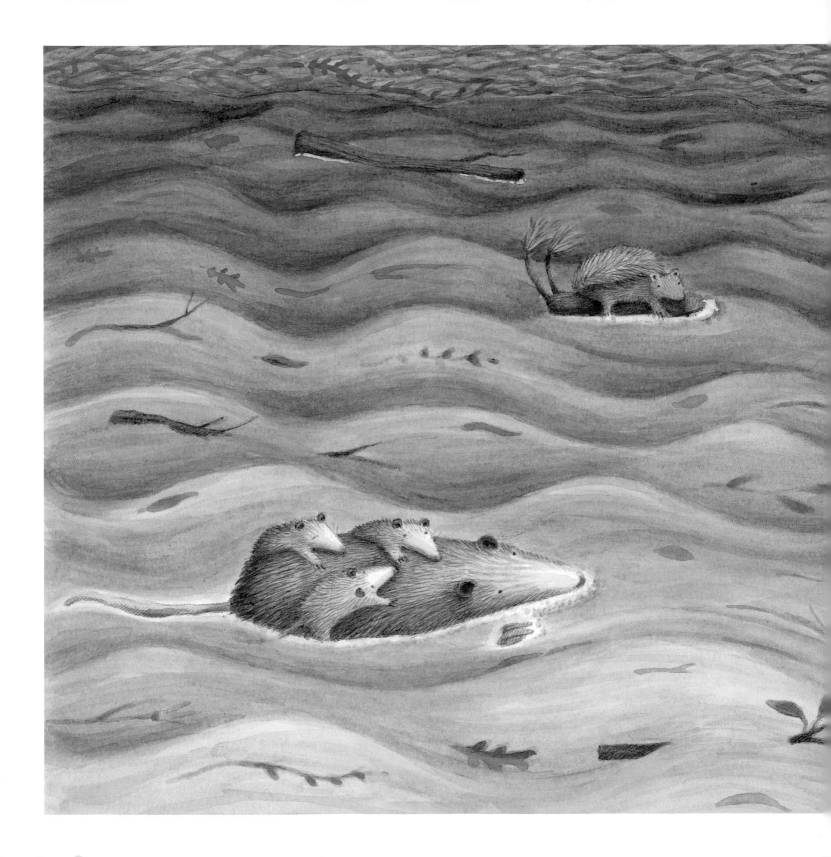

Thunder crashed. Wind howled.
The possum family watched as the
creek rose.

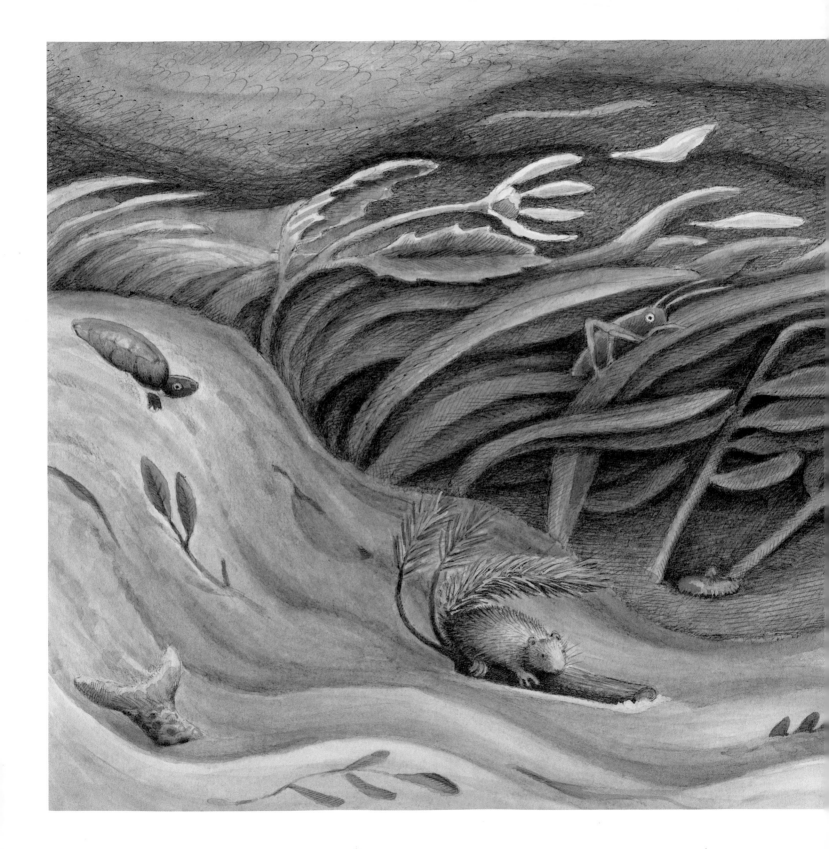

Possum looked out one summer afternoon.

"Time to come in!" he called to his baby possums.

"It looks like we're in for some weather!"

# TO MY EDITOR, MARGARET RAYMO, POSSUM'S OTHER PARENT

www.hmhco.com

The illustrations in this book were done in watercolor and ink.
The text type was set in Minion.
The display type was set in Faith and Glory.

Library of Congress Cataloging-in-Publication Data
Names: Hunter, Anne, author, illustrator.
Title: Possum and the summer storm / by Anne Hunter.
Description: Boston ; New York : Houghton Mifflin Harcourt, [2018] | Summary:
When Possum's brush pile washes away in a storm, his neighbors all help
build a new home based on their own abilities and preferences.
Identifiers: LCCN 2016028101 | ISBN 9780544898912 (hardcover)
Subjects: | CYAC: Dwellings—Fiction. | Opossums—Fiction. |
Animals—Fiction. | Neighborliness—Fiction.
Classification: LCC PZ7.H916555 Pq 2018 | DDC [E]—dc23
LC record available at https://lccn.loc.gov/2016028101

Manufactured in China
SCP 10 9 8 7 6 5 4 3 2 1
4500696763

# POSSUM and the SUMMER STORM

Words and pictures by *Anne Hunter*

Houghton Mifflin Harcourt
Boston   New York

# POSSUM
## and the
# SUMMER STORM